Brookfield
Days

THE COMPLETE
LAURA CHAPTER BOOK COLLECTION

Adapted from the Little House books
by Laura Ingalls Wilder
Illustrated by Renée Graef and Doris Ettlinger

LITTLE HOUSE

Caroline #1

Brookfield Days

ADAPTED FROM THE CAROLINE YEARS BOOKS BY

Maria D. Wilkes

ILLUSTRATED BY

Doris Ettlinger

HarperTrophy ®
A Division of HarperCollinsPublishers

Adaptation by Heather Henson.

HarperCollins®, ☕®, Little House®, Harper Trophy®, and
The Caroline Years™ are trademarks of HarperCollins Publishers Inc.

Brookfield Days
Text adapted from *Little House in Brookfield*,
text copyright 1996, HarperCollins Publishers Inc.
Illustrations by Doris Ettlinger
Illustrations copyright © 1999 by Renée Graef
Copyright © 1999 by HarperCollins Publishers

Library of Congress Cataloging-in-Publication Data
Wilkes, Maria D.
  Brookfield days / adapted from The Caroline years books by Maria D.
Wilkes ; illustrated by Renée Graef. — 1st ed.
    p.   cm. — (A little house chapter book)
  "The Caroline years."
  Summary: Presents the daily experiences and adventures of young Caroline
Quiner, the girl who would grow up to be Laura Ingalls Wilder's mother, in
the frontier town of Brookfield, Wisconsin.
  ISBN 0-06-442086-8 (pbk.). — ISBN 0-06-027952-4 (lib. bdg.)
  1. Ingalls, Caroline Lake Quiner—Juvenile fiction. [1. Ingalls, Caroline
Lake Quiner—Fiction. 2. Wilder, Laura Ingalls, 1867–1957—Family—Fiction.
3. Frontier and pioneer life—Wisconsin—Fiction. 4. Wisconsin—Fiction.
5. Family life—Wisconsin—Fiction.] I. Graef, Renée, ill. II. Title.
III. Series.
PZ7.W648389Br 1999   98-55162
[Fic]—dc21   CIP
                                                                      AC

❖
First Harper Trophy edition, 1999

Contents

CHAPTER 1

Mother's Helper

Morning sunshine peeped through the windows of a little frame house in Brookfield, Wisconsin. Upstairs, Caroline Quiner lay in the big bed she shared with her sisters, Martha and Eliza. She blinked and rubbed her eyes. She wiggled her toes under the sheet and stretched her arms high above her head.

The house was still except for the sound of Mother's brisk footsteps moving across the kitchen floor below. Caroline could hear the fat pork sizzling in the

1

frying pan. She knew that soon the sweet smell of hotcakes would fill the house, and she couldn't wait for Mother to call up the stairs so they could all start the day. Caroline loved helping Mother and making her smile. Especially now, since Mother didn't smile as much as she used to before Father left.

Caroline's father had been gone for almost one whole year. He had sailed away on a big boat, and he had never come back. Mother said Father was in heaven. Caroline missed him very much, and she knew Mother did, too.

Now Grandma lived in the frame house with them and helped Mother take care of them all. Sometimes things were very hard without Father there, but Mother always tried to be cheerful.

"Time to wake up," Mother called from the bottom of the stairs.

Caroline jumped out of bed and gently shook Martha's arm.

"Mother says to wake up," she said.

"Hush, Caroline," Martha grumbled as she pulled the sheet over her head. Martha was the oldest sister. She was eight years old and never liked getting up early.

Just then three-year-old Eliza's eyes popped open. "Up, Martha, up!" she said,

3

and began to bounce on the bed.

Caroline quickly pulled the curtain and tiptoed over to the boys' side of the room. The early-morning air felt cool against her bare feet.

Joseph was the oldest of all the children and Henry came next. They shared a big bed, too. Caroline reached out and shook Henry. He pushed his sandy curls away from his face and sat straight up.

"Morning already, little Brownbraid?" he asked, and Caroline smiled and nodded.

Ever since she was three, Caroline had been called "little Brownbraid." Her father had given her the name. One day, Mother had twisted Caroline's thick, soft hair into one long brown braid. Father saw it at breakfast and said, "How pretty you are, little Brownbraid!" It became his special name just for her.

 4

"Mother says it's time to get up," Caroline said to Henry.

"Then it must be time to get up!" Henry laughed. He nudged Joseph awake, and Caroline turned back to the girls' bed and pulled the curtain behind her.

She was just putting on her own white petticoat and everyday dress when the room began to smell like Mother's hot-cakes. Suddenly, Caroline was in a hurry. She shook Martha's arm once more.

"Wake up!" she called.

Martha threw the quilt back and leaned up on her elbows.

"All right, all right," she yawned. "I'm awake."

Caroline turned around so that Martha could fasten the long row of buttons on the back of her blue cotton dress.

"Hurry, Martha!" Caroline pleaded.

"It's too early to hurry," Martha said sleepily.

Caroline didn't think it was too early. She was too busy thinking about the hotcakes. Hotcakes were her favorite. She loved to drop a pat of butter on the steaming cakes. Then she'd pour sugar syrup over the stack and eat them before the syrup even had a chance to drizzle off the hotcakes onto her plate. Her stomach rumbled just thinking about it.

As soon as Martha was dressed, the three girls rushed downstairs. The kitchen was warm and cozy. Joseph and Henry had already brought the wood in from the woodpile. The fire in the hearth hissed and popped. The sunshine made the room glow with light.

Mother was standing at the hearth. Her straight black hair was neatly pinned

 6

behind her head. She looked up and smiled at the girls.

Grandma was rocking slowly in front of the fire. She had baby Thomas on her knee and she was singing softly to him.

"Good morning, Grandma," Caroline and Martha and Eliza sang out.

"Good morning, dears," Grandma smiled.

Grandma braided each girl's hair, and then they quickly washed their hands and faces at the washstand by the fire. Caroline began to help Martha set the table.

Finally, Mother carried the platters of hotcakes and crisp fat pork slices from the stove to the table. Grandma filled each cup with milk. Martha set a big bowl of applesauce and a crock of butter in the center of the table.

"Bring the sugar syrup, please, Caroline," Mother said, and her eyes twinkled.

Caroline gave Mother her brightest smile. Then she ran to the pantry. When Mother asked her to get the sugar syrup, it meant she could pour it on her hotcakes first—before Eliza and Martha and Henry, even before Joseph! Mother knew just how much Caroline loved sugar syrup.

Back at the table, Caroline set the sugar syrup right next to her plate. She took her seat while Mother said the blessing.

At last it was time to eat hotcakes! Caroline poured out the thick syrup and passed it along. She picked up her fork and took a big bite. The syrup and butter and hotcakes all melted together in her mouth.

When breakfast was done, it was time

 8

to start the morning chores. Everyone had different chores to do. Joseph and Henry went off to chop more wood for the fire. Mother and Martha washed the breakfast dishes.

Caroline was only five years old and too little to wash dishes, but she helped dry each plate and cup. Then she handed the dishes to Martha, and Martha put them back on the dish dresser.

"Time to make the beds and tidy your room, girls!" Mother said and handed the big broom to Caroline.

Caroline and Martha did their morning chores as fast as they could. They were in a hurry to get outside. Caroline knew the chickens were waiting. Feeding the chickens and gathering the eggs was Caroline's special chore.

CHAPTER 2

Outdoor Chores

Caroline and Martha ran outside into the bright morning sunshine. Now that the beds were made and the upstairs room was tidy, it was time for the outdoor chores.

Martha went off to gather acorns and beechnuts to feed the hog, and Caroline headed for the garden. Before Caroline could see to the chickens, she first had to check the corn. It was her job to see if the late-summer ears were ripe yet.

Carefully, she pushed her way through

the first row of tall cornstalks. She searched until she found a thick ear of corn. Mother had shown her how to pull the green wrapping back just far enough to see the first few kernels.

"How does it look, little Brownbraid?"

Caroline turned to find Henry's smiling face peering out between the stalks.

"Is it ready yet?" he asked.

Every morning Caroline checked on the corn. And every morning Henry waited at the end of a row and asked the same question. Henry loved the buttery sweet taste of corn just as much as Caroline did.

"I think it's still a little bit too small," Caroline called out.

"Maybe by the end of the week!" Henry shouted back, and his sandy curls disappeared behind the stalks.

Caroline smoothed the leaves back up

over the kernels and hurried to the barn. Sunlight flooded through the big barn doors as she ran inside. The smell of fresh cut hay filled the air.

Caroline found her egg basket and a wooden bucket in the back room. She picked them up and headed for the grain bin.

The grain bin was made of wood, and it stood almost as tall as Caroline. Joseph and Henry kept it filled with grain to feed the horses and the cow and the pig and the chickens.

Caroline set the bucket and basket on the ground next to the bin. Caroline knew she should ask her brothers to help her lift the lid, but she wanted to lift it herself. With all her might, she tried to lift the top of the bin high above her head and push it against the wall. But it was just too heavy.

The lid dropped shut with a big *bang*!

"Wait just a minute, silly!" Henry shouted as he ran into the barn. He reached above Caroline's head and flung the top of the bin open. "A little one like you can't swing that top so high," he scolded.

"It's just a little bit heavy," Caroline answered back. "I almost did it."

Caroline reached into the bin to fill her bucket. The soft bits of grain tickled her hands and made her fingers dusty and fresh-smelling. When the bucket was half full, Caroline picked up the empty basket and rushed back out into the late-summer sunshine.

The tiny henhouse was nestled up against one side of the barn. A wooden peg kept the henhouse door closed snug and tight during the night. Caroline twisted

 14

the peg and let the door drop gently to the ground. The door made a nice little slope for the hens to walk down.

"Morning, hens!" she called. "Sorry it took me so long, but I had to check the corn before I came to feed you. It's still not ripe."

The hens poked their brown- and gold-feathered heads out of their house. Then they hopped down the open door, fluttering their wings and squawking loudly as they went.

Caroline took a handful of grain from her bucket and began to scatter it in a circle in front of the henhouse.

"Here's your breakfast, hens," she called. "I had hotcakes and sugar syrup this morning."

The hens waddled and squawked. Their red crowns bobbed up and down as

15

they picked at the kernels of grain.

"You're not talking to those silly hens again, are you?" Martha was standing behind Caroline, holding a bucket full of nuts. "You don't think they'll talk back, do you?" she teased.

"Course not!" Caroline said. "I just wonder what they're saying to each other, that's all."

"Oh, Caroline!" Martha laughed. "Mother's waiting for the eggs. Hurry and take them to the house."

"I'll hurry," Caroline said. She tossed the last handfuls of grain onto the ground. Then she clapped her dusty hands together and peered through the henhouse door. "Let's see how many eggs we have today."

Ever so carefully, she reached inside and ran her fingers through the straw.

One, two, three. Four. Five! Five eggs!

Caroline almost shouted with delight. Five eggs! Mother would be so happy!

Caroline left the eggs safely in their boxes for a moment. She tugged some tall grass from the ground and made a small green nest in her basket. Then she took each egg out of its nesting box and cushioned it in the soft grass.

The hens were just finishing their breakfast. They clucked and flapped their wings and strutted on the dirt floor.

"Thank you, hens," Caroline sang out. She looked inside her basket again. She still couldn't believe it. Five whole eggs! She smiled proudly and hurried back toward the house, holding her basket of eggs tightly. She couldn't wait to show Mother.

CHAPTER 3

Wash Day

The next day was Monday. Monday was the day that Mother did the washing. Caroline helped Martha carry buckets of water from the well to the house, while Mother heated the water in a big kettle on the fire.

Carrying water was hard work because Mother needed a lot of water to do the washing. All morning long, Caroline and Martha carried bucket after bucket from the well. The bucket's wooden handle dug into Caroline's fingers. The water jumped and splashed from one side of the bucket to the other. The yard seemed to grow bigger with each trip. Caroline thought she would never reach the house.

Martha trudged along beside her sister. Her bucket was much bigger than Caroline's. With every step, Martha's bucket tipped and sloshed. The water drenched her apron and the grass around her.

"When I'm a grown lady," Martha said. "I'm going to have so many dresses, I'll never have to wash them! I'll just wear a different one every day."

Caroline tried to think about having so many pretty dresses, but all she could think about was her aching fingers.

"Do your fingers hurt, Martha?" she asked quietly. She didn't want Mother to hear her complaining.

"My fingers . . . and my hands, and my arms!" Martha answered loudly. She didn't mind Mother hearing one bit.

When they finally reached the house, Mother took the buckets and poured the water into the big iron kettle.

"Thank you, girls," Mother said brightly. "That's all the water I'll need right now."

Martha let out a loud sigh. Caroline kept quiet, but she was glad the hauling was over. Her arms tingled, and her fingers were stiff. Even her back hurt a little.

Now it was time to check the wood box. Mother needed plenty of wood to keep the fire leaping beneath the big iron pot. The water in the pot must keep boiling for as long as she washed clothes. Time after time during wash day, Mother reached into the wood box for more wood. It was

Martha's job to make sure the box was full.

When the water in the pot was steaming and bubbling, Mother asked Caroline to sort all the clothing into two piles on the floor.

"One pile should have all the white clothes," said Mother, "and the other should have all the colored clothes."

Caroline sat down in the middle of the floor. The pile of dresses and trousers, skirts and blouses, socks and long underwear towered over her head. As quick as she could, she sorted all the clothes into two piles.

"Now you can hand me the white clothes, one at a time," Mother told her.

The washtub was full of soapy bubbles. Caroline handed Martha's apron to Mother and watched as Mother plunged it into the washtub and pulled it out, dripping and

21

covered with suds. Mother then spread the apron on the ribbed washstick and scrubbed as hard as she could.

When Mother had finished scrubbing every piece of white clothing, she carried them all to the hearth and dropped them one by one into the pot of boiling water. She stood over the iron pot and stirred the clothes with a long stick.

Finally, she took the long stick and lifted the clothes out of the hot, soapy water. She carefully dropped them into another, empty tub.

"I'm almost ready for the colored clothes," Mother said, wiping her brow.

Caroline carried all the dark trousers, the blue- and brown- and red-print dresses, and the flannel socks and shirts to the tub of soapy water. She began handing each piece to Mother, just as she had done

with the white clothes.

The soap squeaked and squished as
Mother scrubbed the wet clothes against
the ribbed wood of the washstick.

"Now it's time to empty this tub,"
Mother said when all the dark clothes
were scrubbed and clean.

Joseph and Henry came in from chop-
ping wood. They carried the steaming
iron pot outside and tipped it over in the

grass. Soapy water gushed out onto the ground.

Mother took a rag and wiped the inside of the iron pot clean. Then the boys carried the pot back into the house and set it over the fire.

Now it was time to carry water again. Caroline didn't tell Mother how much her hands hurt. She helped carry as many buckets as she could back into the house. Her fingers were red and burning when the iron pot was finally full again.

As soon as the water in the pot began to boil again, Mother said, "Time to rinse the clothes."

Caroline watched as Mother rinsed first the white clothes and then the dark clothes in the boiling water. When Mother was sure everything was rinsed clean, she pulled the clothes out of the pot with the

 24

long stick. Then she twisted and squeezed each piece over the empty pot, wringing out as much water as she could.

"Goodness glory, these baskets are heavy today," Mother said as she carried the clean clothes outside. Her face was pink from the heat. Long strands of her black hair had escaped from her bun and were pasted against her forehead and neck.

Outside, Mother pulled the clean clothes out of the basket and shook each piece a final time. The clothes snapped loudly and a spray of water droplets flew into the air. Caroline helped find a soft grassy spot to lay each piece neatly to dry.

"I suppose we'll have to let the sun finish the job now, won't we?" Mother asked, looking around at all the clean clothes drying on the warm grass.

Caroline nodded her head. Beneath her bonnet, she could feel the heavy heat of the sun. She knew the clothes would dry quickly.

Mother's eyes sparkled down at Caroline. "You've been such a big help today," she said. "I think we just may have to use some of those fine eggs you gathered yesterday to make a special treat for after supper."

Caroline smiled and tucked her hand into Mother's. As they walked together across the yard, Mother gently squeezed Caroline's fingers, and the fingers didn't feel quite so sore anymore.

CHAPTER 4

Early Frost

The summer sunshine began to ease into fall. Then one morning, there was a chill in the air as Caroline checked on the corn and fed the chickens. That night at supper, Mother's face was full of worry. She told them all in a solemn voice that they must prepare for an early frost.

"First thing in the morning, we must bring in the rest of the vegetables," Mother said. "A frost could ruin them, so we need to store them for now for winter."

"Are all the vegetables ready to be

27

harvested, Charlotte?" Grandma asked.

Mother shook her head. "No, but it's a risk we'll have to take, Mother Quiner," she answered. "Better to have vegetables that are not yet ripe than no vegetables all winter long."

Caroline looked at Henry and then down at her plate. She thought about all the sweet ears of corn in the garden. She wondered how Mother knew about the early frost, but she didn't want to ask.

Mother turned to Caroline and her face softened. "This will be your first time helping us harvest, Caroline," she said. "And now we'll especially need your help."

Caroline felt her cheeks turn pink with pride. Mother's words made everything a little better.

As soon as supper was over, Caroline

and Martha quickly dried the dishes and put them away. Henry and Joseph went to refill the wood box. When they opened the door a sudden blast of cold air rushed through the house.

"Goodness glory!" Mother cried. "I had no idea how much colder it was getting." She looked anxiously into the dark, and then closed the door tightly.

On most nights the children sat around the fire and listened to Mother and Grandma tell stories. But tonight they kissed Grandma, baby Thomas, and Mother and quietly went upstairs.

"Be certain to put your quilts on your beds," Mother called after them. "And put on your flannel nightclothes."

Caroline could feel the cold air creeping up the stairs. She shivered, thinking of the cold night and day ahead. As quickly as

she could, she put Eliza into her flannel nightgown. Eliza's teeth chattered as Caroline tied her nightcap strings under her little chin.

"Hurry under the covers, Eliza," Caroline said kindly. "It will be much warmer there."

As soon as Eliza was tucked beneath the quilt, Caroline quickly pulled on her own nightgown. She could hear the wind howling at the window, and she could feel the cold air sweeping across the hard wood floor. Shivering all over, Caroline jumped in next to her sister.

"It's too cold to harvest all those vegetables in the morning," Martha whispered as she scrambled into bed.

Caroline didn't say a word. She snuggled deeper beneath the quilt, but she could still feel the cold in her toes, fingers, and cheeks. She couldn't imagine picking all those ears of corn in the cold daylight. But she knew she would have to try her best for Mother.

CHAPTER 5

First Harvest

"Wake up, girls," Caroline heard Mother say in a quiet voice. Caroline opened her eyes and saw Mother's gray wool dress with the little white buttons that climbed all the way up to her chin. Mother's hair was already neatly tucked beneath her bonnet, but her eyes weren't cheerful. They were tired.

Caroline sat up and looked around the room. Her nose and toes and fingers ached with cold. Suddenly she remembered the garden. Mother was supposed to wake them before the sun rose so they could pick the vegetables. But the room was already bright with daylight.

"Are we going to pick the vegetables now, Mother?" Caroline asked, as Martha and Eliza woke up and rubbed the sleep out of their eyes.

"No, Caroline," Mother said in a weary voice. She explained that the frost had come even earlier than they had thought it would. She and Joseph had woken up in the middle of the night. They had picked as many vegetables as they could before the frost settled.

Mother looked around at them and gave her brave smile.

"Don't worry," she said. "Remember we have all the potatoes, turnips, beets, and onions that are still under the dirt, protected from the frost. When it warms up this morning, we'll all go out into the garden and see what's left. Perhaps we didn't lose so much to the frost after all."

On her way down the stairs, Mother added, "Make sure you dress warmly, children."

The cold air nipped Caroline's fingers as she took off her nightgown and put on her flannels and wool dress and stockings. She even put on her shoes, now that it was so cold.

As she dressed Eliza, Caroline glanced around the room. Something was strange. Every morning, the sunshine made the little room glow. But this morning, the room was filled with a hazy white light. The windows weren't letting any golden beams through their glass panes.

Caroline looked more closely at the windowpane.

"Oh, Martha!" she cried. "Come look!"

The glass was covered by thick white frost. Its swirls and diamonds and snowflake patterns were delicately dusted all over the window.

Caroline gently touched the bottom corner of the windowpane with one fingertip, and the frost began to melt. Caroline peeked outside through the tiny circle.

The sun was shining bright in a glassy blue sky. The outside was a dazzling world of white. The trees, the roof of the henhouse, the split logs in the woodpile, the corn and squash and tomatoes in the garden—everything was covered by an icy white blanket.

Martha squeezed in next to Caroline

 36

and looked outside.

"It looks so cold," she cried.

"I want to see! I want to see!" Eliza jumped up and down on the floor behind them.

"Pretty!" she cried when Caroline picked her up and held her to the window. She pressed her little nose against the glass. "Cold!" she wailed and buried her face in Caroline's shoulder.

"Girls!" The sound of Mother's voice sent the sisters running down the stairs to breakfast. Grandma and Mother had already set the table and gathered all the chairs.

The roaring fire made Caroline forget the cold for a little while. The sweet smell of toasted bread filled the house.

Mother placed a piece of toast on each plate. She poured a steaming hot sauce made of milk and butter and flour all over the browned slices of bread. As Caroline ate, the hot milk-toast warmed her all the way down to her toes.

When breakfast was over, Mother said that they would do the dishes, but that the rest of the chores would wait until later.

"We need to find out if there are any vegetables that survived the frost in the garden," Mother said.

Soon the last dish was dried and put back on the dish dresser. Caroline wrapped her shawl snugly around her head and shoulders and followed Mother outside. The cold air stung her cheeks and filled her lungs. The sun sparkled over the frozen-white yard. The brightness brought tears to the corners of her eyes.

Caroline picked her way carefully through the frosted grass. When she saw the garden, her heart sank. The tomato vines were black and droopy. The squash and the pumpkins had a thick white covering. The tall stalks of corn were now hunched over under the weight of the frost.

The frost had seemed so beautiful to Caroline from the upstairs bedroom. But now she saw how ugly it really was. It killed their vegetables before they ever had a chance to finish growing.

"Can we still pick anything?" Caroline asked.

Mother stood in middle of the garden, silently looking around. Then she abruptly turned to Joseph and Henry and told them to bring every basket and pail they could find out of the barn.

"We will pick every vegetable we can find, children," she said in a firm voice.

"We worked too hard to keep these plants growing. We will find something to do with every one of these vegetables."

Mother's words cheered everyone. They all bustled about. Caroline almost forgot the cold as her fingers flew across the droopy vines and plants.

By the time every basket, crate, and pail was filled with vegetables, the warm sun was high in the sky. The frost began to melt and drip to the earth from the leaves and branches.

Caroline looked down at the cold, wet earth and the piles of dead vines and plants. Today was the first time she had ever helped harvest. Now her back ached from bending over the frozen vines and her arms hurt from picking so many squashes and tomatoes. Her fingers were stiff and cold.

 40

"What will we do with all the vegetables that are not yet ripe, Mother?" Martha asked.

"We'll wash and peel them," Mother answered, and her voice became more hopeful as she spoke. "After we finish slicing them, we'll cook them with vinegar and spices, and some salt and pepper. We may not be able to eat them as they are, but we'll be able to have tomato, squash, and pumpkin pickles all winter."

"Pumpkin pickles!" Henry cried. "Whoever heard of pumpkin pickles?"

"No one yet," Mother admitted, "but the girls will help me make them while you boys dig up the rest of the vegetables."

Caroline clapped her tired hands together. She was happy that she didn't have to do any more digging. And she couldn't wait to help Mother make pumpkin pickles. The cold, terrible frost hadn't ruined everything after all.

CHAPTER 6

Two Birthdays

Drifts of snow soon hugged the rooftop of the little frame house. A thick white frost covered the windowpanes. Winter had come to Brookfield.

Each night, after the supper dishes had been wiped and put away, the whole family sat together around the cozy fire. The boys played checkers while Mother did her mending. Caroline and Martha practiced their sewing, and Grandma watched Eliza and baby Thomas.

Caroline was working on a sampler.

43

Sometimes Grandma helped her finish a difficult stitch. Caroline would sit on Grandma's lap and watch as Grandma's gentle hands covered her own. Together, they would pull the needle through the stiff cloth.

Mother always sang while she did the mending. Caroline loved to listen to her soft voice go up and down over a pretty melody.

One night, Mother caught Caroline's eye as she finished a song.

"I believe it's almost time for your birthday, Caroline," Mother said.

Caroline let out a little gasp. "When will my birthday be, Mother?" she asked.

"Let's see," Mother answered, counting to herself. "Just four more days."

"But I thought I didn't have a birthday," Caroline said.

 44

Mother eyes opened wide. "Why, of course you do. Whatever makes you think that you don't?" she asked.

Caroline knew that Martha had birthdays, and so did Joseph and Henry. Even Thomas and Eliza had birthdays. She often wondered how she had turned five without a birthday, but she never asked Mother.

Grandma glanced up from her needlework. "We didn't celebrate Caroline's birthday last year," she said in a quiet voice to Mother. "We had just received the news."

Mother's face became sad, and all at once, Caroline wished Grandma had never said those words. She remembered the day they had heard that Father was not coming home ever again, and she wanted to cry.

"I remember now," Mother said softly.

She knelt down in front of Caroline and looked into her eyes. "We didn't celebrate your birthday last year because we were all too sad for a celebration. But this year we aren't sad, Caroline. As a matter of fact"— she clapped her hands together—"this year we'll celebrate two birthdays. Five and six!"

Mother's happy face made Caroline forget her tears. She clapped her hands, too, and put her arms tightly around Mother.

Two birthdays! Caroline had never heard of such a thing. She didn't think she could wait four whole days.

Each morning, Caroline rushed through her chores, trying to make the day go faster. Each night, she closed her eyes, happy that her birthday was one day closer.

Finally, on the morning of her birthday, Caroline crept out of bed before the sun was even up. The room was silent as she tiptoed about, trying to dress herself as quietly as she could. She brushed her hair until it shone and hurried downstairs with her blue hair ribbon.

Grandma and Mother were just beginning to make breakfast.

"My goodness, Caroline!" Mother exclaimed when she saw her. "It is very early for you to be up. Today must be a very special day!"

"Yes, Mother," Caroline answered shyly. She hoped it was still her birthday.

"Hurry and wash your hands and face," Mother told her.

As Caroline carefully washed her hands and face, the smell of breakfast cooking began to fill the kitchen. Caroline

47

suddenly felt very hungry.

"Are you making hotcakes, Mother?" Caroline asked hopefully.

"Why, of course, Caroline. Today we're celebrating two birthdays!" Mother's smile spread from one side of her face to the other. "Come, let's braid your hair and get you ready."

Caroline held her blue ribbon out to Grandma like she always did, but Mother said quickly, "I'll braid your hair today, Caroline."

Mother sat on a chair behind Caroline and began twisting and pulling her hair into one long brown braid.

As Mother's fingers neared the bottom of her braid, Caroline handed her the blue hair ribbon.

"Oh, Caroline," Mother said, "you cannot wear such an old ribbon on your

 48

birthday. You need something bright and new to begin a new year!"

Mother spun Caroline around. Caroline eyes opened wide when she saw a new dark green ribbon lying in Mother's open hands.

"Oh, Mother," Caroline said. "It's so beautiful."

"Happy birthday number five!" Mother laughed and tied the ribbon in a smart bow around the bottom of Caroline's braid.

Caroline was so busy admiring her new ribbon, she almost didn't see Mother reach inside her apron pocket. She pulled out a small bundle wrapped in a swatch of tan cloth.

"Happy birthday number six, Caroline," Mother said.

Gently Caroline unfolded the cloth.

Inside she found a beautiful rag doll. Black button eyes sparkled in the early-morning light, and a red yarn mouth smiled up at her. Curly black yarn hair was pulled back into a braid that fell down the doll's plaid dress. The braid was tied at the end with a tiny dark green bow that matched Caroline's new bow.

Caroline lovingly smoothed the doll's dress and touched her pretty bow.

"Oh, Mother," she whispered as she pressed the rag doll's little face against her cheek. "My very own doll! I shall call her Abigail."

"Grandma helped me make Abigail," Mother said. "You must thank her, too."

Caroline hurried to hug Grandma as Mother finished making breakfast. Soon the whole house smelled like hotcakes.

While she waited for the day to begin, Caroline held Abigail tightly with one hand and kept reaching behind her back with the other. She wanted to be certain that her new green bow was still safely wrapped around the bottom of her braid.

Only a few short days ago Caroline didn't think she had a birthday. Today she was having not just one birthday, but two. And Mother had given her the best presents she could have ever imagined.

CHAPTER 7

Good Friends

Winters were always long and hard in Wisconsin, but this winter seemed to be the longest and hardest of them all. The days were short and cold. At night the bitter wind rattled the windows.

For weeks a heavy snow fell. When Caroline peeped outside, everything was buried under a thick blanket of white. Worst of all, there was very little food in the house. There were no animals in the forest for Joseph to hunt, and the supply of vegetables in the cellar was getting low.

In the mornings, there were no more hotcakes. There were only small bowls of cornmeal mixed with water and a pinch of salt. Henry called it "Mother's mush." Caroline didn't like mush at all, but she was so hungry, she could have eaten two bowls of it every morning, maybe even three. But Mother cooked only enough for one bowl each.

One morning, after the breakfast

dishes had been wiped and put away, Caroline was helping Martha tidy the upstairs. First she helped make the beds. Then she plumped the pillows. She was on her way down the stairs to get the broom, when she saw Joseph and Mother standing by the door. Joseph's coat and hat were covered with fresh snow.

"We didn't find anything," Joseph told Mother. "Every trap was empty."

"We'll just have to see what's left in the root cellar, Joseph," Mother said, and Caroline could hear the worry in her voice. "We've gone without meat for longer than this."

"I'm going to help Henry clear the snow from the woodpile," Joseph said. He pulled the flaps of his coat tightly together beneath his chin and opened the door.

Brilliant sunshine and a blast of cold air

rushed into the kitchen. Mother closed the door tightly behind Joseph. When she turned, her face looked sad. But when she saw Caroline standing on the stairs, she smiled her bright smile.

"I was just coming down to get the broom," Caroline said.

Mother nodded and Caroline hurried to the corner to fetch the broom. She was just about to go back upstairs, when suddenly there were three loud thumps— *bang, bang, bang*—at the kitchen door.

Caroline's heart began to pound. She rushed to stand behind Mother.

"Gracious!" Mother cried.

Caroline peeked around Mother's skirt as Mother pulled open the kitchen door. Sunlight rushed back into the room. Two tall figures stood in the doorway. Caroline couldn't see their faces because of the brilliant glare from the sun and snow.

Joseph stepped into the kitchen. Caroline saw a large hand resting on his shoulder. Mother moved swiftly forward.

"What's wrong, Joseph?" she cried. "What's happened?"

Joseph's mouth opened. But instead of Joseph's voice, Caroline heard a very deep voice speaking in a strange rush of words.

Mother stepped back, startled. Caroline looked from Mother's face back to the doorway and gasped. A large man stepped into the room in front of Joseph. Caroline realized that the strange voice belonged to an Indian.

The Indian's eyes were black and sparkling. Thick black hair fell down around the shoulders of his tan leather coat. A scar stretched from the corner of his left eye all the way down his cheek to the side of his chin. His large hands moved in the air as he nodded and spoke to Mother quickly.

"What is it?" Mother asked in a voice Caroline had never heard before.

"Don't be afraid, Mother," Joseph said. "This man is Crooked Bone. You met him once with Father. When Father took us hunting, Crooked Bone often found us in the woods and showed us how to set traps and kill game quickly."

Mother did not move, but Caroline could feel her relaxing a little.

"I do remember him now," she said. "But what does he want, Joseph? Does he know that Father isn't here?"

Joseph nodded his head. "He knows, Mother. And he brought us meat. More meat than even Henry could eat!"

"Meat!" echoed Crooked Bone. "Bring

here!" He pointed to the floor beneath his snowy boots and then shouted to someone outside.

Before Mother could say a word, a second Indian entered the room. He too had long black hair that hung straight down around his face and shoulders. His forehead was damp with sweat. He was pulling with all his might on a rope that stretched out the door.

"Wait!" Mother cried. "Please wait!"

Huffing and puffing, the second Indian struggled forward. Caroline peeked around Mother and saw that a large deer was attached to the end of the Indian's rope. Frosty white patches of snow and ice were caked on its fur.

Mother went silent. Her eyes were wide and unbelieving. She looked from the deer to the Indians and exclaimed,

 58

"This is for us? The whole animal?"

Crooked Bone clapped his hands together and smiled.

"See boy in forest," he said, pointing to Joseph. "Trap is empty for many sun, many moon." Crooked Bone shook his head and pointed to the buck. "Hungry. Friends must eat. Good friends."

Mother looked up at Crooked Bone. "Thank you," she said. "Thank you."

Crooked Bone nodded and then spoke to his friend. The two men stepped outside to help Joseph drag the deer across the yard and into the barn.

Mother shut the door behind them. When she turned around, Caroline saw that her eyes shone with tears that didn't fall.

CHAPTER 8

A Winter Feast

Caroline ran up the stairs so fast that she was out of breath when she reached the top. Her head spun thinking about Crooked Bone and his wonderful gift. Suddenly, she felt very hungry.

"We have meat, Martha!" Caroline cried. "The Indians came. Father's friends! They brought us meat—a whole deer! Come downstairs. We have to help Mother."

Martha turned to Caroline, her eyes round as saucers. "Oh, Caroline, I missed

60

it! Are they still here?"

"They're going to the barn with Joseph and Henry," Caroline answered.

The girls clattered down the stairs. Now Mother was cheerful and busy. She stood in front of the fire, poking the logs with a black iron stick. Orange and gold sparks popped out of the wood from all sides and soared up the chimney.

"We need a brisk fire to cook all that meat," Mother explained.

Just then Henry burst through the door with the first piece of fresh venison.

"Here it is!" he shouted.

Mother hung the venison over the fire, then she placed a shallow pan directly beneath it. Caroline watched as Mother stood before the hearth, carefully turning the meat.

"Such a treat!" she cried. "We must be

sure to cook it evenly!"

After turning the meat, Mother stoked the logs. A flurry of sparks flew out. Drops of juice began to drip into the basting pan as the meat slowly cooked. Carefully, Mother pulled the basting pan from the fire with a long pair of iron tongs. She poured the drippings back over the meat.

"Such a treat!" she said again. "We mustn't let it get too dry."

Soon Henry and Joseph and the two Indians came back into the house with the rest of the venison. Martha watched the Indians with wonder. For once, she didn't say a word.

Caroline saw that the last of the meat was cut into thin strips. Crooked Bone walked over to Mother and showed her the strips he held in his hand.

"Keep long time," he said.

"Cook it on the fire?" Mother asked.

"Cook slow," said Crooked Bone. "Dry and keep long time."

Crooked Bone began hanging long pieces of twine from the wooden mantel above the hearth. His friend tied strips of meat to the twine. The front of the hearth was soon covered with chunks and strips of meat slowly roasting and drying.

"So much meat!" Mother said. She stood back and admired all their hard work. "We'll have enough until spring, if we use it sparingly."

Mother turned to the girls. "Martha, bring me an onion from the cellar," she said. "And Caroline, put a tiny bit of flour into a small bowl and bring it to me. We must make these drippings into gravy."

Gravy! Caroline's mouth watered just thinking about it.

Mother turned back to Crooked Bone and his friend.

"Will you stay for supper?" she asked.

Crooked Bone shook his head and pointed toward the door. "Crooked Bone go. Friends eat."

"Thank you for your kindness," Mother said, and Caroline saw that her eyes were full again.

"Friends," Crooked Bone said in his deep voice, and then the two men were gone.

When supper was finally ready, it was dark outside the windows. The meat strips hung before the crackling flames in the hearth, cooking slowly. The warm house was filled with the musky smell of roasted venison. The plates on the table were piled high with meat, corn, bread, turnips, and gravy.

 64

Caroline bowed her head as Mother said the blessing. She knew they had so much to be thankful for that night.

CHAPTER 9

Welcoming Spring

Caroline tapped her feet restlessly on the floor beneath her chair. She put her sampler down on the sewing table and crossed over to the window to peer outside at the gloom.

Dark clouds had chased all the blue from the sky. A cold, steady rain had been falling for days. It seemed to Caroline that winter would never end.

"Do you think spring will ever come, Grandma?" she asked.

"Of course it will, child," Grandma

answered. "You must have patience."

Caroline sighed softly. She couldn't wait for the world outside the window to be green instead of gray. She wanted to run and play in the warm sunshine.

Mother came to stand beside Caroline. She looked out at all the grayness, and then she looked back at Caroline.

"I think we need a celebration!" she said, and her eyes sparkled.

"A celebration?" Martha asked, dropping her knitting. "What will we celebrate, Mother?"

"We'll celebrate springtime," Mother answered brightly. "We'll welcome the spring."

"Welcome spring!" Eliza cooed, throwing her little arms up in the air and waving them around.

Caroline and Martha and Eliza all

rushed to follow Mother into the kitchen.

"How will we celebrate?" Martha asked.

Mother looked down at the stove thoughtfully. "Well, we have a fine dinner stewing already," she answered. "Still, a fine dinner isn't enough for such an occasion. We must make a treat for our celebration. Something simple but special."

The girls watched as Mother placed two eggs, a spoonful of salt, and a small bowl of flour on the table.

"We can make some delightful cakes with this," Mother said.

While Mother started the grease melting on the stove, Martha carefully cracked the eggs into a bowl. Caroline and Eliza watched Martha beat the eggs until they were light and fluffy.

Mother came back from the stove and

 68

sprinkled the top of the beaten eggs with a pinch of salt. She beat the egg mixture for a little while longer and then she reached for the bowl of flour.

"It's your turn, Caroline," Mother said, scooping up a small amount of flour in a ladle. "While I stir, please sprinkle the flour slowly over the batter."

Caroline held the ladle as carefully as she could so that none of the flour would spill over the sides. Slowly, she dusted the top of the eggs with flour while Mother kept mixing. She added more flour until the batter was too stiff to beat.

"Thank you, Caroline," Mother said. "That will be plenty."

Mother pushed the dough together until it formed a round ball. Then she kneaded it quickly. She tossed a sprinkling of flour over the top of the table and pinched little pieces from the big ball of dough. She handed one piece each to Caroline, Martha, and Eliza.

Mother showed them how to roll the pieces between their palms until they had each formed a perfect little ball. On the table top, she flattened the dough balls until they were very thin. Then she slowly peeled each one up from the table.

"Time to check the grease," she said, peering into the pan on the stove. The hot lard was sputtering and popping.

Mother began to drop the flattened balls into the pan one by one. Caroline and Martha stood on tiptoe and watched. Each little cake was immediately surrounded by tiny bubbles as it fell into the pool of hot fat. The cakes sizzled and fried and swelled into big doughy puffs that floated to the surface of the pan. Within a minute

or two, every cake had turned a golden
brown.

"They look so lovely, Mother!" Martha
cried.

"What do you call them?" Caroline
asked.

"Why, I don't rightly know, Caroline,"
Mother smiled.

"Puffcakes!" Martha suggested.

"Golden puffballs!" Caroline cried.

"Perhaps we should taste them first, and then decide exactly what to call them," Mother suggested.

"When can we eat them?" Caroline asked.

"We'll set them down to cool while we eat dinner," Mother answered, "and they'll still be warm and crunchy when it comes time for dessert."

"But Mother," Caroline worried, "how can we eat the cakes before Henry and Joseph come home?" Now that it was almost spring, Henry and Joseph went to school each day. They didn't come home until after dinner.

"We'll save each of them a cake," Mother said. "They just won't get to eat them when they're warm, like we will!"

Caroline and Martha hurried to gather plates and cups from the dish dresser.

Mother carefully lifted each cake out of the hot lard with a long-handled spoon. Then she set it on a flat tin that was covered with a clean rag.

For dinner, there were steaming bowls of venison stew and warm cornbread. When the bowls were empty, Caroline helped Martha clear the dishes and wipe them and put them carefully away.

"Now we'll have our celebration," Mother said cheerfully as she served the cakes around the table.

The little cakes were still warm and crunchy. Caroline bit into hers, and she thought that it tasted like a bubble might taste: light and airy and quick to disappear. She slowly savored each bite.

It wasn't until later that night when she lay in bed that Caroline realized they had never named the cakes. But that didn't matter. The cakes were delicious just as they were.

Caroline fell asleep that night feeling warm and full inside, and dreaming of sunshine and soft, green grass. The winter had been long and hard, but spring was on its way.